County Kerry,
west coast of Ireland, 1830.
Bitter tears were shed,
and a ring was thrown.

For Carolyn. Us. 50 years

Poesy rings, in use from the Middle Ages,
were given for friendship and love.

First published 2018 by Walker Books Ltd
87 Vauxhall Walk, London SE11 5HJ

10 9 8 7 6 5 4 3 2 1

Copyright © 2018 Blackbird Design Pty Ltd

The right of Bob Graham to be identified as author and illustrator
of this work has been asserted by him in accordance with
the Copyright, Designs and Patents Act 1988

Printed in China

British Library Cataloguing in Publication Data:
a catalogue record for this book is available from the British Library

ISBN 978-1-4063-7827-6

www.walker.co.uk

WALKER BOOKS
AND SUBSIDIARIES
LONDON · BOSTON · SYDNEY · AUCKLAND

THE POESY RING

Love never dies

BOB GRAHAM

The poesy ring flew high, caught by the wind.
And with the breeze in its tail,
the horse turned and galloped.
Salt tears dried on the rider's face.
The ring tumbled end over end,
and settled deep in a meadow near the sea ...

and there the ring stayed with just
small creatures to keep it company
as the seasons slipped on by.

Storms blew in from the ocean.
Sand and salt flattened the grass.

Moons passed many times overhead.
And the stars fell from the sky.

In time, the ring was joined by an acorn

that dropped from a hole in a small boy's pocket.

The ring and the oak became close neighbours,

and like a big wheel the seasons kept turning...

A fawn was born in the spring,

and ate acorns dropped by the oak in the autumn.

Wedged tight into the deer's cloven hoof
was the poesy ring, and written inside, "Love never dies".

Once more in the meadow looking across the sea,
the ring flew through the air.

In that meadow,

the ring found a feather bed ...

unseen by the reaper!

Years went by, then the earth peeled and folded,

and with the soft thud of the surf, and the screeching of gulls ...

the ring surfaced again
into the light.

It left the ground and lifted high
in the air...

From a
startled beak,
it dropped ...

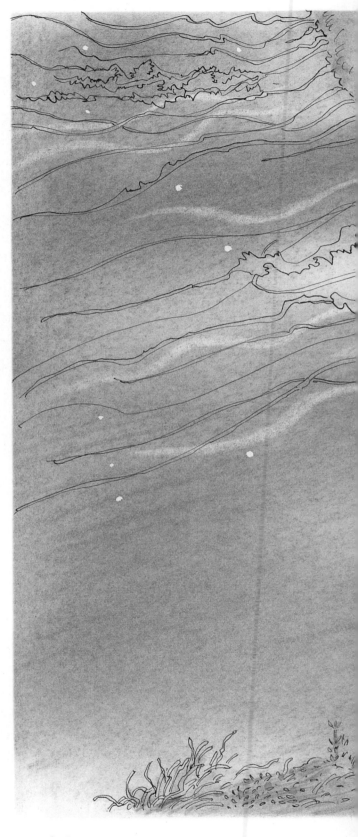

deep to the bottom of the sea.

Washed by countless tides.

Seen only by generations of passing fish.

Sunken sea treasure on the ocean floor.

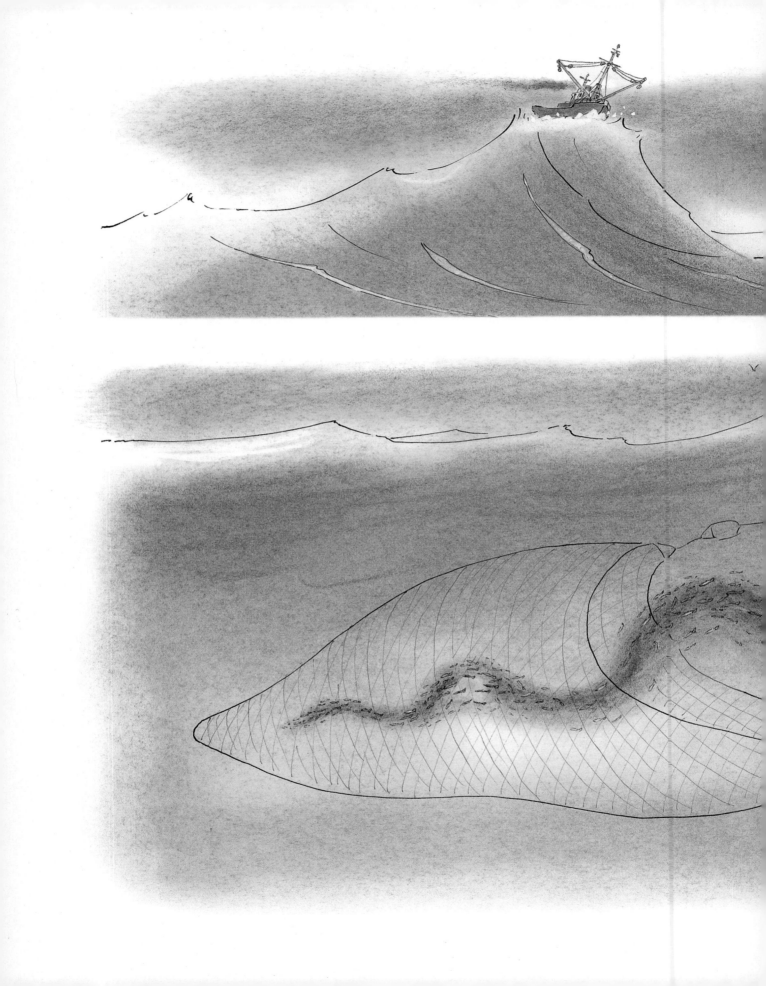

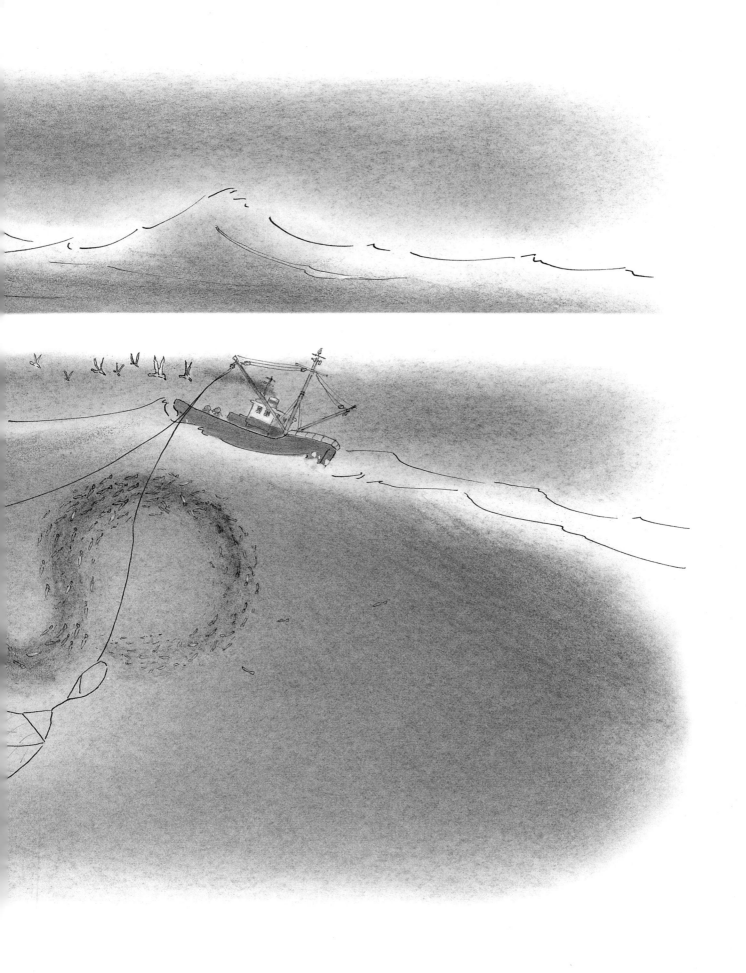

A treasure at last found ...

and sold!

In a windy subway station,
Sonny and Jules finished their day's work.

With money in their pockets
they went up to the street.

1967

New York City, Lower East Side.
It was winter.

And the ring found a finger.

They bought hot chestnuts on 23rd Street.

And the Salvation Army brass band played hymns on the corner.

Then Sonny and Jules walked home in the snow.